The Author's Presence in the Select Fictional Elements of Osamu Dazai's No Longer Human

Louren Jay Caballero
Dr. Lito Diones
Mark Paul Famat
Christia Mae Rodriguez

Ukiyoto Publishing

All global publishing rights are held by

Ukiyoto Publishing

Published in 2023

Content Copyright © Louren Jay Caballero, Dr. Lito Diones, Mark Paul Famat, Christia Mae Rodriguez

ISBN 9789360163488

All rights reserved.
No part of this publication may be reproduced, transmitted, or stored in a retrieval system, in any form by any means, electronic, mechanical, photocopying, recording or otherwise, without the prior permission of the publisher.

The moral rights of the author have been asserted.

This book is sold subject to the condition that it shall not by way of trade or otherwise, be lent, resold, hired out or otherwise circulated, without the publisher's prior consent, in any form of binding or cover other than that in which it is published.

www.ukiyoto.com

Dedication

To all the lovers of literature, may this symbol of perseverance bless you with creative wonder and spirit. To those dreams yet fulfilled, this is a sign to never stop in your pursuit of self-fulfillment. To poets and writers in mind, keep writing, keep crafting, keep discovering, and keep searching for your own voice. All can be attained at the right time of God.

Acknowledgements

We would like to give merit and express our deepest gratitude to the people who have made significant and impactful contributions that have spelled success for this research paper.

First and foremost, we extol and praise our Almighty Father for bestowing upon us enough perseverance, determination, strength, knowledge, and wisdom to successfully and duly accomplish this research paper.

To our research adviser, Dr. Lito L. Diones, who painstakingly and patiently guided us, along with his unwavering support and assistance in the process of making this paper. His perceptive and astute suggestions and remarks during consultations were enormously valuable in the fulfillment of this paper.

We would like to express our profound appreciation to our parents, students, and friends, whose love, support, and encouragement have been palpable from the outset.

Finally, thanks to the literary researchers for persevering through the difficulties of this long and difficult journey. Our sense of collaboration, determination, and optimism unified us to gain success.

Abstract

This study investigates the author's presence in the select fictional elements of Osamu Dazai's No Longer Human, which specifically delves into the plot, characters, and milieu. The data which supports the study is obtained using two literary theories, namely Abram's Expressive Theory as the primary theory, which mainly relates the author's life, beliefs, and experiences to its literary works, and Guerin's Historical-Biographical approach as the supporting lens to find latent connections between the author's literary works and the author's historical and social conditions in which the author lived. Moreover, this study is qualitative in form, using discourse analysis as the method to analyze the literary work exhaustively. The findings of the study show that the plot evidently manifests the author's real-life events and experiences; the similarities of the characters in terms of traits match Osamu Dazai; the events of Oba Yozo and Dazai's timeline prove that the author's milieu influences the development of his literary work. In conclusion, Osamu Dazai's novel No Longer Human reveals the author's presence. Furthermore, it is recommended to conduct an extensive exploration of the structural development of the plot using other plot models; probe into the characters' psychological aspects, especially their motivations, desires, and influences that drive depravity; to conduct an in-depth investigation into the different kinds of milieu and its relevance to the theme of the literary work.

Keywords: author's presence, japanese literature, fictional elements, no longer human, expressivism.

Contents

The Problem And Its Scope	1
Review Of Related Readings	9
Literary Research Methodology	18
Presentation, Analysis, And Interpretation Of Data	22
Summary Of Findings, Conclusion, And Recommendations	42
About the Author	*51*

The Problem And Its Scope

Rationale of the Study

A world without literature is a realm barely existing. To live life without music, art, and poetry is like living without a purpose. Since time immemorial, people have started documenting experiences throughout their lives which lead to the rise of literature.

Literature is a collection of diverse stories, which people hear from generation to generation. Stories that present the origin of civilization, stories that portray the life of society, stories that hold catapults of emotions during the wars, stories that reflect an identity after independence, and stories that share a soul to the world. The modes of expression varied according to experiences, time, place, and civilization.

Plays, short stories, songs, poems, and novels play an essential role in society as these mediums of writing express shared experiences, emotions, and stories to other people. With that notion, authors are the ink of all the pages in their stories as they are the primary source and the core of their literary works.

Osamu Dazai is one of the most notable writers, ranking his novel entitled "No Longer Human" as the second best-selling novel in Japan. In his preface to the English translation, Donald Keene discussed the Japanese novel's literal translation: Disqualified from Being Human (Post Magazine).

One of the many kinds of literature is a novel which is primarily lengthy narrative prose that tells a story. During the process of literary creation, it is inevitable for a writer to incorporate a portion of its identity in its works which may come in the form of the person's writing style or a close depiction of the author's real-life experiences. The mentioned notions that were incorporated in the works would then become a manifestation of the author's presence.

Literary elements such as plot are one relevant approach to detecting the writer's occurrence in his creations. The plot is the series of interwoven events in a piece of literature, tale, drama, memoir, or narrative that reveals the lead linkages between the events that take place in the narration. It is the process of escalating and resolving a conflict. The significance and interconnections of the writer's real-life experiences are noted to be incorporated in their literary work through this chain of events.

The character drives the story as a whole. It plays the role in a narrative and creates various types of conflicts and tensions as well as different types of resolutions. More often than not, the characters in the story can be based on an author's pure imagination, or sometimes related to real individuals, in which case the dichotomy between a real and fictional character can be evaluated.

Every story has a milieu. A milieu is basically a chronological timeline of significant happenings in the story. It is made up of people, emotions, places of action, or in which a story takes place.

With the interest in how an author's presence is revealed in his work, the study affirms that somehow it is inevitable for the author to separate himself, entirely, when writing a literary piece. Specifically, with the definition, literature is also a form of indirect confession of one's feelings, emotions, and experiences. An author and his literary work possess a connection, and it is called the author's presence. The author's presence can be seen in any literary work by scrutinizing its literary and fictional elements.

In this matter, the purpose of the study is to investigate the author's presence with the use of plot, character, and milieu to answer the main problem.

Theoretical Background of the Study

The study assumes that Osamu Dazai's No Longer Human reveals the author's presence.

The assumption of the study is being supported by Meyer Howard Abrams' Expressive theory as the main theory and Guerin's Historical-Biographical approach as a supporting theory.

Expressive Theory

Expressive theory primarily focuses on the relationship of the author's life and his works of literature. It thoroughly examines the writer's experiences, beliefs, and political, sociological, and economical context to gain a better understanding of the text.

In Abram's Glossary of Literary Terms, expressive criticism treats a literary work primarily in relation to its author. It defines poetry as an expression, overflow, or utterance of feelings, or as the product of the poet's imagination operating on his or her perceptions, thoughts, and feelings; it tends to judge the work by its sincerity, or its adequacy to the poet's individual vision or state of mind; and it often seeks in the work evidence of the particular temperament and experiences of the author who, deliberately or unconsciously, has revealed himself or herself in it. This theory views how one demonstrates his experiences through his crafts towards his audience or readers as a product of his emotions. In some way, it is unavoidable for an author to impart a portion of his identity in his literary piece because an author can subconsciously associate his experiences during the process of the literary pieces.

4 The Author's Presence in the Select Fictional Elements of Osamu Dazai's No Longer Human

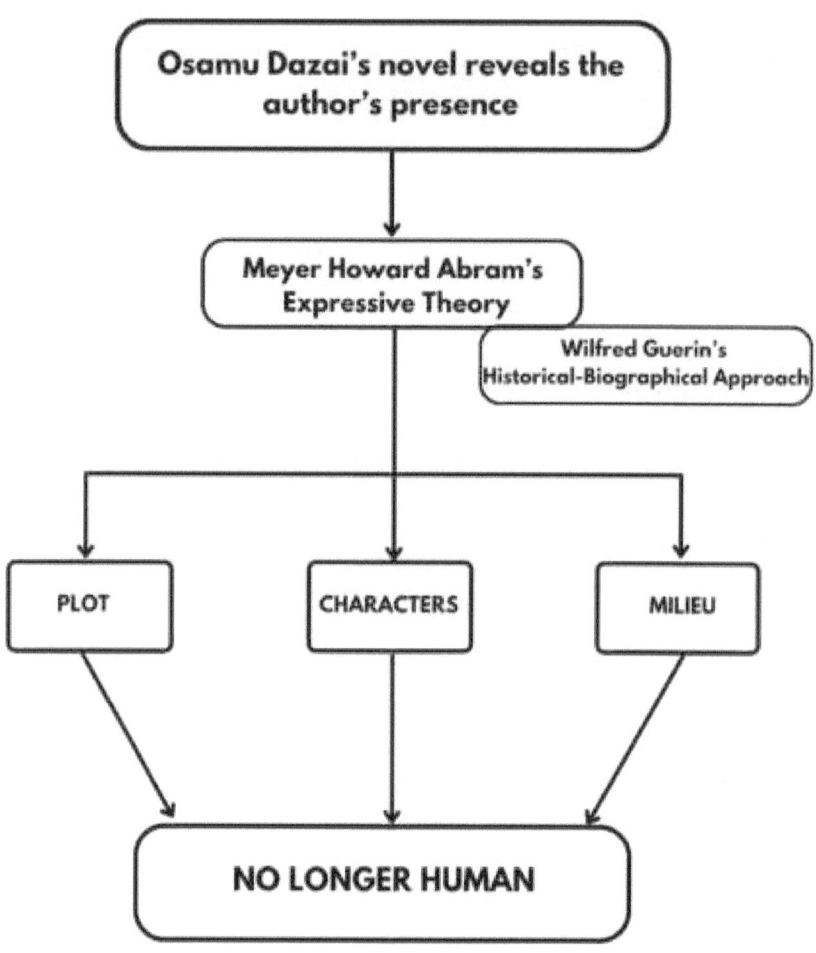

Figure 1. Schematic Presentation and Conceptual Background of the Study

At the core lens of expressive criticism, the author's presence could be excavated hidden between the lines that constitute the storyline or plot of the narrative. The plot refers to the interconnected events that reveal the cause-and-effect relationships between one event and the other that happened in the story. On the account of these series of events, the influence and connection of the author's life experiences may be embedded in one way or another in the plot of the story.

In studying the author's presence in a novel using Expressive Criticism, the character represents a portion of the author's personal life. These fragments of the author's presence are seen in the character's physical appearance, mannerisms or behavior, and upbringing. These above-mentioned characteristics may or may not coincide with the actual experiences of the author.

The use of Expressive Theory in the conduct of this study serves as a key finding of the remnants of the author, for it criticizes a literary work as a product of human real-life experiences and beliefs. This theory critically pins down the signs of the author's identity, which can possibly be located or revealed in the plot, characters, and milieu.

Historical-Biographical Approach

Through a significant lens, historical-biographical theory interprets a literary work that centers the connection between the author's personal life experiences, beliefs, values, identity, and amongst others and the components that comprise the author's literary pieces. Moreover, it inspects how the plot, characters, and settings of the literary piece mirror or represent a picture of the actual culture in which the author lived. Explicitly, it somehow perceived a literary work as an imitation of an author's life.

According to Guerin, historical-biographical approach sees a literary work chiefly, if not exclusively as a reflection of its author's life and times or of the characters in the work.

This approach intends to comprehend a literary text by examining the historical and social circumstances of the time and milieu in which the work was written. It certainly encompasses an understanding of the world the author lived in. Through the scrutiny of the milieu in which the novel was made, the author's presence may be discovered using the historical approach. Milieu refers to the surrounding culture or setting in which a particular art has emerged. It involves the people, culture, and current societal situation.

In the biographical lens in examining comprehensively a literary work concerning the author's presence, this theory inspects the author's identity; gender, class, race, family history, sexual orientation, political position, ethnicity, educational background, and nationality. On the other hand, the historical lens investigates primarily the historical, cultural, and intellectual context. In simpler terms, both theories examine the relationship between the author and his work, taking into significant consideration the life and the times of the author and looking to see how these elements are related or revealed in the work.

Due to the fact that it takes into account the author's history and biography, the historical-biographical method as a sub-theory contributes significantly to the main theory's support. With the help of the ideas provided by the sub-theory, the research can examine the similarities between the author's life and the novel's storyline, characters, and setting, among other things.

Problem Statement of the Study

This study investigates the author's presence in Osamu Dazai's "No Longer Human". Specifically, it looks into:

1. Plot;
2. Characters; and
3. Milieu

Significance of the Study

This study is beneficial to those who are interested and inclined in the discipline of literature, specifically students, teachers, and researchers who want to explore the realm of literature to expand their knowledge and gain new information. Also, it is even more substantial for literary enthusiasts who aspire to engage in Japanese Literature. This study will not just give them an introduction to the culture, history, and literature of Japan but an overture to the life of Osamu Dazai and his literary work and style of writing. Moreover, profound ideas on investigating the author's presence are conferred in this study. Finally, the generated information of this research will contribute as a future reference to studies related to the author's presence and Dazai's life and literary works.

Scope and Limitations of the Study

The scope of the study is focused on investigating the author's presence in the novel "No Longer Human" by Osamu Dazai translated by Donald Keene which was published by New Directions Publishing Corporation in the year 1973. The story is interpreted using expressive theory as the main theory and historical-biographical theory as the sub-theory.

The limitations of this study are within the parameters of the sub-problems raised, specifically the plot, characters, and milieu.

Definition of Terms

The following words are defined operationally to give a clear cut on the use of these terms in the study.

Author's presence is also referred to as an authorial presence. It denotes some signs about the life of the author that was imparted in particular literary elements in his literary work.

Realm Barely Existing is a situation of a place that is scarcely living a blissful life because literature is non-existent in its place.

Indirect confession refers to the author's truths that were written in a non-obvious manner.

Semi-Autobiographical (of a literary piece) is partly influenced by the events of the author's personal life with the integration of fictional elements

Review Of Related Readings

This chapter reviews some readings that relate to and support the main research problem and its sub-problems.

Review of Related Literature

In order to support and strengthen the ideas of the study, the researchers gather parallel and relative literatures that deal with the author's presence in the plot, characters, milieu, and theories.

In an essay scrutinizing Jack London's To Build a Fire, the plot reflected on the author's life specifically Jack Landon's struggles while living in the snowy environment he was in. The same findings were also found in the characters of the story ("Biographical Criticism…").

This essay presented a concrete instance where an author's life is reflected or revealed in his literary work. This benefits the study as to where to locate the author's presence with regard to its fictional elements.

Malaran also made a demonstration about the application of the historical and biographical approach in his presentation "Historical and Biographical Approach". It was Jose Rizal's "Noli Me Tangere". In his example, he demonstrated that some of the characters were a reflection of the people during Jose Rizal's time. According to him, Cristomo Ibarra was a reference to Filipinos who were able to get an education abroad, Padre Damaso reflected the abusive priests yet was referred by then, Kapitan Tiyago being the Filipinos who had to make ties with the authorities for their own sake and Sisa and her children were referenced for the oppressed Filipinos by the Spaniards ("Historical and Biographical Approach").

Malaran discusses certain parts of the story to show the relevance of the milieu in the production of a literary work. The narrative and characters in Osamu Dazai's "No Longer Human" will be examined to see if they represent Dazai's milieu.

Goad made an article, "How Far Do Authors Reflect Themselves in Their Protagonists?", discussing how authors put a portion or perhaps their whole personality in their works. According to the author, writers such as Oscar Wilde and Ernest Hemmingway were apparently represented by a certain character in their works such as Wilde being represented by Basil Hallward in "The Picture of Dorian Gray". Also discussed were authors who impart a small portion of their own selves to their readers, allowing them to live vicariously through their characters, such as Aldous Huxley, who was represented by the characters Bernard Marx and Huxley in the novel. ("How Far Do Authors Reflect Themselves…").

The authors who affirmed their presence in their works opened the path for the study's premise of locating the author's existence in its literary creations. It ensures that the narrative's characters are connected to the author's own story, if not fully.

Furthermore, an essay also made the same approach to its respective literary piece being studied, namely "The Story of an Hour". According to the essay, the main character of the said story Louise Mallard bore similarities to the novel's author, Kate Chopin. An example of the said similarity was the death of the main character's husband which may have been a reference of Kate Chopin's mother being widowed. The author's milieu may have also been another factor as to why the literary piece was conceived. During the author's time, women were not as valued to the point that they were deprived of their rights towards education, property, and other privileges ("Biographical Approach to Kate Chopin's".)

Similar to Kate Chopin's short story, the resemblances of the author are observed between the character and the plot of the story revealing a portion or a hint that links to the author's presence.

Rossen also talked about the different authors who incorporated their own selves in their crafts. Examples include Philip Roth who wrote himself in his book "Operation Shylock: A Confession" where both the author and the one in the book both suffered a nervous breakdown due to a sedative. Rossen also featured W. Somerset Maugham who also put himself in his works such as

"Human Bondage", and "The Razor's Edge" to interact with his characters such as giving advice in times of existential crisis ("7 Authors Who Wrote Themselves").

This list of authors who wrote stories according to their life offers an affirmation that some writers write stories based on their life stories and experiences. Similar to the study, it deals with associating an author's personal life with his literary creation may it be intentional or unintentional.

Moreover, Tikaocta investigated the presence of the author in the characters of Edgar Allan Poe's "The Black Cat". He used biographical criticism to reveal the similarities of thought, experience, and feelings expressed by the author in the literary work. The author's main goal was to find references to the writer's life, education, and socio-cultural environment in the piece. By the end of the analysis, the author concluded that "The man's character (the narrator) in the story has the same character as Edgar Allan Poe. Both of them married early, had pets, and are alcoholics. Poe reflects on some parts of his life in his short story "The Black Cat". Thus, the life of the author clearly affects the work that he wrote (Historical-Biographical Approach).

The study clearly shows that the author's real-life character may have a huge possibility to reflect on the character of the story that he wrote. This serves as a reference to examine the influence of the author on the characters of Osamu Dazai's novel.

In an online article, it stated that every writer has his own imagination but more likely they gather stories from their personal experiences or their memory. In the process of writing, it is inevitably inescapable for writers to attribute their personal beliefs or philosophy in life, which reflects the characters' behavior or personality in the story. He also provides famous authors who have reflected their experiences in their literary works such as Harper Lee who looked back to her memories and relived them by writing them, and Martin Luther King Jr. who imparted his dreams and experiences.

Moreover, he also presented Maya Angelou as one of the writers who referenced their literary creations and masterpieces according to the significant events of her life that remain as moments and memories of the past. In addition, the article claimed that literature brings back old memories and opens up wounds of the past as literature is a reflection of human experiences. In conclusion, the author asserts that literature is truly a reflection of one's life and experiences ("The Reflection of Literature").

Literature is a collection of different stories, adventures, journeys, and lessons. It bestows everyone with a platform to express themselves through writing. With that notion, any literary piece could be a reflection of someone's identity, personality, and desire.

In the article "The Art of the Semi-Autobiographical Novel by Emily Temple", she presented a list of literary works that were written semi-autobiographically such as We the Animals by Justin Torres, who admitted that he created the story and the characters from his own life, and Go Tell It on the Mountain by James Baldwin, who declared to have based the story from his experiences as a teenage preacher in a small church in Harlem, and amongst other novel written semi-autobiographically - wherein the characters in the story are based on the author's personal life experiences ("The Art of the Semi-Autobiographical Novel").

With that concept, writers can truly write in a variety of styles in order to express the message they wish to portray. Sometimes, the story is inspired by other people's personal narratives but most of the time; it came from the author's personal life experiences, thoughts, and imaginations that reflect the author's presence in the process of creating a literary piece.

In the article of Tahir Wood, he presented the semantics of fictional characters within an extensive framework of authorial communication. Moreover, he discusses that the theories of character in the novel will be incomplete to the point that characters are not realized as enthused creations of an author. He also argued that the sentiment of the typical character should preferably be observed as a relation concerning the figure-grounding creation of characters and the social milieu of the authorial presence (Research Gate).

Since the characters of the stories are the products of an author's imagination, there are high chances that the behavior, personality, milieu, or plot of the story provides a hint to link the characters to the author. Moreover, this article benefits the study in locating the author's presence in the social milieu.

Cole et. al. probed into William Golding's "Lord of the Flies" using the biographical approach. In the study, several events in the plot reflected the author's life experiences. The coincidences were inspired by the time when he participated as a naval officer during the Second World War (the milieu he was in) which is said to have developed a change in his outlook on life, specifically, a darker and more realistic one. The said outlooks were also applied to the values of his writing in the novel ("Applying Biographical Criticism").

The study proves that the milieu the author was living in may influence the author in molding his/her literary work. On that note, the author's presence could still be found in the milieu of the story.

Review of Related Studies

In Lianne J. M. Boer's work, she used the concept of plot to demonstrate how regional and global legal experts use their work to guide readers toward a certain conclusion about the meaning of the law. Additionally, she used Peter Brooks's book Reading for Plot, which defines plot as "the structure and purpose of the narrative, what forms a story and gives it a particular direction or intent of meaning" (11). To establish the writer's presence in the text, she began with a metadiscourse analysis, which examines the components of a text in which writers reveal themselves, such as those of the statement "In this section I shall argue." In conclusion, the examination of metatext aided in elucidating the plot's purpose as evidence of the author's presence. Correspondingly, in linguistic analysis of academic writing, both the first and third person pronouns ('the present writers') are referred to as self-mentions that indicate the author's presence. The writer's obscurity is self-imposed, and in that setting, it provides as much confirmation of her identity as her overt written appearance would (20).

This study asserts that the presence of the writer may manifest in the plot of the text that exposes a part of the writer's real-life events.

Further, this study will help the researchers to identify the events of the author's life in his art.

Margaret H. Freeman conducted a study of authorial presence in poetry. She stated in her paper that the presence of the author in poetry may take several forms depending on the reader's perceptions. The author asserts that most of the previous studies in criticism have dealt with issues regarding the inferences readers make of an author's identity, attitudes, and moral positions; questions of reliable or unreliable relations between narrator and author (implied or historical); and a lot more problems associated with discerning authorial presence (1). In addition, Freeman also stated that readers understand authorial presence in literature in at least two ways. She pointed out that some make direct connections between the writer's life and literary works; others distance the writer's real, "historical" self by invoking an authorial self or poetic persona (202).

Freeman testifies how readers understand the authorial presence in literature. She meant to point out that the presence of the author in poetry may occur in various ways depending on the perception of the reader.

As stated in the study of Navrativola, authorial presence is the degree of visibility and authoritativeness that writers show in the text in revealing their attitudes, judgments, and assessments. Further, according to Ivanic, The degree of visibility and authority that writers chose when building an authorial voice relies on the interplay of many internal and external factors that are connected with the facets of the identity of the author that interact in academic discourse. That is the autobiographical self, the self of discourse, and the authorial self (1).

In Navrativola's study, he explored the use of author-reference pronouns for the explication of authorial presence in the genre of research articles in the field of linguistics. The analysis showed that the author-reference pronouns have significant means of showing the author's identity, despite the influence of scientific paradigms that instruct objectivity and avoidance of the author's personality in academic writing. The findings revealed in the field of applied linguistics, a tendency towards a more subjective way of expression has been strongly developed over the past decade (30).

Eefje Claassen investigated the role of the author in the mind of the reader. She provides empirical evidence that some readers do in fact construct images of a real-life author. Her studies support the theory that some readers make a default judgment, "that the author is a morally acceptable person." Regardless of whether they know anything about the historical author, the findings of her study suggest that interpretations about the author play a crucial role in the course of literary reading (1).

This study demonstrates how readers construct images of the real-life author in the characters of the story regardless of the author's background. It shows that readers assume that the author is present in the characters of the writer's work.

Pakenier also tried to look for the author's presence in Vladimir Maiakovskii's books for children. What Pakenier found about Vladimir Maiakovskii was that Maiakovskii was an avant-garde poet meaning the styles in making the art was unconventional, unusual, or experimental (1). The study concluded that the children and the significance of him was apparent, which denotes that only to children did Maiakovskii reveal and present himself as "Uncle House" genuinely and sincerely (910).

This study proves that a certain art style applied in the making of art can also serve as an author's presence because it reflects on its maker.

Sarig conducted a study about the author's presence found in certain literary pieces. In it, the author assumed that a.) an author's presence, rather than it being a direct confession of the realities experienced by the said author, it was more of a "poetic artifact" and b.) readers can actualize the author's presence once they feel it. The author raised while conducting his study that the author's presence has six qualities, specifically sincerity; self-revelation; creativity & innovativeness; intensity; interactivity, and use of poetic devices. After probing the study, the author concluded that in the set of literary pieces the author studied, the quality of self-revelation was the most common quality found (1).

This study will aid the paper as to what qualities of the author's presence in this Osamu Daza's "No Longer Human" will be discovered.

Furthermore, in a study conducted by Tang and John, the authors claimed that the first-person "I" was not fixed to a single entity in terms of meaning. They conducted their study in the essays of the first-year undergraduates to do so. To carry out their study they created a spectrum consisting of 6 different identities in relation to the first-person pronoun "I", specifically the "I" as a "representative", "guide", "architect", "opinion-holder", and "originator". The degree of authorial presence ranged from least to greatest respectively (29).

Tang and John's work will help the study identify what sort of an author's presence resides in Osamu Dazai's "No Longer Human".

Mark Fenster also tried to find the author's presence, specifically David O Selznick's, in the movie "Since You Went Away" thus conceiving the study "Constructing the Image of Authorial Presence: David O Selznick and the Marketing of Since you Went Away". In his study, he found that Selznick's influence was more on the promotion and the production of the movie and not on the theme and the style that shaped the movie. The author's findings were supported when he stated what Selznick wrote to Gallup during that time and that Selznick's central intention was to "make the film as successful as possible"(49).

This study testifies that a person's actions that will influence the development of work of art, (in this case, a movie) may also serve as an author's presence. Moreover, this helps to intensify and amplify in proving the author's presence.

In Lyon's "Art is Me: Dazai Osamu's Narrative Self as a Permeable Self", the author viewed Osamu Dazai's Narrative Voice as that of something that can be seen through or transparent. His claim was supported by his finding in various literary works of Osamu Dazai whose characters and voice that constituted them were as if telling the readers to merge with the Dazai and his thoughts. An example of it was his analysis of the main character of the novel "The Setting Sun" where he presented an excerpt from the novel. In it, it was a scene of

Kazuko (the main character) spoke of her thoughts and emotions due to being heartbroken, a scene where the main character "opens" herself up making the readers feel as if they were the character herself (93).

This is a strong affirmation that can support the assumption of this study as it delves into the search for Osamu Dazai's voice associated with his works of literature. Moreover, it was apparent that some episodes of his life were reflected in his work.

According to Suzanne Ferguson in her paper about authorial presence, she stated that the authorial presence in third-person impressionist has two aspects; indirect reporting of speech and thought in the free implicit style and over-intervention. She also suggested how authorial presence constructs characteristics of impressionist effects of ambiguity and irony and should divulge a classic impressionist narration (230).

This study supports that the authorial presence is possible to reflect on the literary pieces of the author, especially in the narration of the characters that could link to the author's personality and life stories.

Literary Research Methodology

This chapter discusses the method and procedure undertaken to solve the problem and sub-problems under study through literary investigation.

Method of Literary Research Used

This study is a qualitative research that makes use of discourse analysis through Expressive Theory and Historical-Biographical Theory which focus on investigating the author's presence in Osamu Dazai's No Longer Human. The qualitative method involves descriptive and non-numerical methods that provide an in-depth interpretation of data. Discourse analysis is a research method that aims to examine the contextual meaning of language in a literary work. This study primarily focuses on the analysis of the literary piece to address the main problem and the sub-problems.

Sources of Data

The primary source of data is the novel No Longer Human by Osamu Dazai translated by Donald Keene and published by New Directions Publishing Corporation in the year 1973.

The secondary sources of data are accumulated from electronic sources including online journals, dissertations, and articles that are relevant to the topic being addressed.

Data Gathering Procedure

In gathering the data, the procedure of the study undertakes the following three phases: Phase 1: Plot, Phase 2: Characters, and Phase 3: Milieu.

Phase 1: Plot

The plot constitutes of different arrangement or sequence of interconnected events of the story. In this first phase of the study, the events in the novel are the vital components in order to uncover the connection of the author to his literary work. In investigating this element, the story's events and the author's life are both significant variables to identify the author's presence with the use of historical-biographical theory. The data are presented in one table analysis using the Aristotelian Linear Plot Model.

Table 1: Author's Presence in the Plot

PLOT	AUTHOR'S PRESENCE
Beginning	
Middle	
Ending	

Phase 2: Characters

The characters are the personas that execute the actions or dialogues of the story that has different personalities, behaviors, and appearance. In this second phase of the study, the characters in the novel of Osamu Dazai's No Longer Human are the substantial elements to investigate the similitude of the author's identity in locating the author's presence with the use of the expressive and historical-biographical theories. The data are presented in one table analysis.

Table 2: Author's Presence in the Characters

CHARACTERS	AUTHOR'S PRESENCE

Phase 3: Milieu

The milieu is a hybrid element that completes the setting of the story. It is a timetable that composes of the mood, historical background, physical and social environment, and place of action in the story. In this final phase of the study, the milieu will go through a thorough analysis to determine the resemblances of the timeline in the author's life scenarios with the use of the historical-biographical approach. The data are presented in one table analysis.

Table 3: Milieu

MILIEU	AUTHOR'S PRESENCE

Data Analysis

This study applies a qualitative discourse analysis method. This method requires descriptive data presentation, interpretation, and analysis of the study under investigation. It examines and interprets primary and secondary sources of data to gather information essential to answer the main and sub-problem of the research. In addition, the three (3) phases are probed and explored using the lens of Expressive Theory as the principal theory and Historical-Biographical theory as the sub-theory.

Ethical Consideration

The study, being qualitative in form, follows ethical principles and exclusively used discourse analysis. Hence, neither person nor animal was involved during the conduct of the study. Due to the fact that there were no respondents involved, no animal or human rights were disrespected. The works involved coming from different authors were also appropriately quoted and acknowledged. Lastly, Osamu Dazai, the author of the novel involved in the study has departed. Due to this reason, it was unnecessary to ask for permission from the deceased author.

Presentation, Analysis, And Interpretation Of Data

This chapter analyzes, interprets, and pinpoints the shreds of evidence that prove the author's presence is in the plot (series of events), characters, and the milieu.

Plot

Below is Table 1 which presents the author's presence in the plot specifically events related to the author.

Table 1. Author's Presence in the Plot

PLOT	AUTHOR'S PRESENCE
Beginning Oba Yozo grew up in an affluent family in the Northeast village and was raised by relatives and his servants. He then eventually grew distant towards everyone around him.	He belonged to a wealthy family.
	He grew up in the Northern part of Japan.
	He was raised by his Aunt Kiye and family servants.

Middle His education deteriorated and his whole life went downhill after meeting Horiki, his corruptive friend, as he got lost in drinking, prostitution, morphine addiction, and suicidal attempts.	He developed vices after the death of his favorite author's death, Ryunosuke Akutagawa, such as drinking, hiring prostitutes, morphine addiction, and eventually becoming mentally unstable and suicidal.
	He left the university without a degree.
	He enrolled in French Literature but did not attend any lectures.
Ending His spiraling life had him to be eventually hospitalized and rehabilitated in a mental asylum making him feel alienated and invalid as a human. He was later isolated in a house in the countryside bought by his elder brother.	He was hospitalized.
	He developed an addiction to a morphine-based painkiller.
	He was rehabilitated to a mental institution and was enforced to resign from his addiction.
	His elder brother assumed parental responsibilities after his father's death.

As shown in Table 1 above, these are the significant events related to the author's life in the development of the story. At the beginning of the narrative, Oba Yozo grew up in an affluent family in the Northeast Village somewhere in Japan and was fostered by his relatives, and family servants because his parents are usually absent at home as his mother was barely mentioned in the scenes of the book. Whereas his father, an influential politician in their town, often have meetings and prior commitments to attend to with his political undertakings, as clearly narrated on page 29 and 36 respectively:

> "My father frequently had business in Tokyo and maintained a townhouse for that reason. He spent two or three weeks of the month at a time in the city, always returning laden with a really staggering quantity of presents, not only for members of our immediate family, but even for our relatives. "

> "A celebrated figure of the political party to which my father belonged had come to deliver a speech in our town…"

As Yozo grew up, he began to feed his curiosity with unusual things that a child would do in which he strangely gets fascinated by the idea of it which made him create his own façade and wear a mask of his personality which caused him to be distant with people. One time in his class, he submitted a doleful story to his teacher just so he can appear as a mischievous child. This particular scenario was oddly blissful to him, clearly narrated on page 35:

> "I had succeeded in appearing mischievous. I had succeeded in escaping from being respected…"

Having his own little world, he spent most of his time in solitary doing his personal pastimes such as reading and writing. With the mentioned events in the life of Oba Yozo, the same thing also happened to Osamu Dazai as a child. Based on Dazai's biography, it stated that he was born in a wealthy family in the Northern Part of Japan where he was raised by his Aunt Kiye and family servants as his politician father, Gen'emon Tsushima, resided most of his time attending political affairs while his mother, Tane, was ill and afflicted customarily. With the absence of both parents, Dazai also wanders his childhood life feeding himself things that interest him such as reading magazines and literary volumes ("The Famous People").

The similitude of events circulating at the beginning of Oba Yozo's life evidently manifests the life of Osamu Dazai's reality as the series of events mentioned seemingly mimic each other and project a parallel motion of narration. It is truly possible that authors do reveal themselves in the series of events of their own literary creations. As stated by Boers in her study, she concluded that the plot is the manifestation of the writer's presence as it shapes the narrative of the story, and it also provides detailed significances that reveal the presence of the author in the accounts of the story or in the presence of the text (20).

Furthermore, in continuation with the development of Oba Yozo's life, in the central or middle happenings in his life as adulthood, Yozo's life demonstrates his personal obstacles and dilemma as his life escalates drastically in motion influenced by his dark and depressing idea in masking his own identity and his belief being a human.

As presented in the table above, in the middle narrative, Oba Yozo's life drifted to a severe extent that his education deteriorated and got doomed by his personal socialization issue as he becomes distant even more to everyone around him because of the existential crisis happening and clashing inside him. Having made his pretentious self and conveying himself with his fraud buffoonery, he began to embody it as a reality and not merely a desire. With his disguised self, he starts to become his true identity, as accurately accounted on page 42:

> "One might attribute this, perhaps, to the fact that my clowning had by this time become so much a part of me that it was no longer such a strain to trick others. I wonder, though, if it was not due instead to the incontestable difference in the problem involved in performing before one's own family and strangers, or in one's own town and elsewhere."

Along with the corrosion of his identity, his education followed in the slope of the landslide as he started to wander in a meaningless path when he met Horiki, one of his fellow artists. He got lost with no direction to vices such as drinking, prostitution, morphine addiction, and several suicidal attempts. On page 58, he said that Horiki encouraged him to engage in the mysteries of drink, cigarettes, prostitutes, pawnshops, and left-wing thought. This series of events was strongly accounted for as well on page 72 of the book:

> "To make the round of the bars with Horiki, drinking cheap sake wherever we went. I almost completely neglected both my school work and my painting. Then in November of my second year in college I got involved in a love suicide with a married woman older than myself. This changed everything. I had stopped attending classes and no longer devoted a minute of study to my courses; amazingly enough I seemed nevertheless to be able to give sensible answers in the examinations, and I managed somehow to keep my family under the delusion that all was well."

There were two significant suicides Yozo attempted, the first was when he met a bar waitress and they both decided and agreed to commit suicide by drowning themselves in the sea of Kamakura. Unfortunately, the desire of Yozo to die failed as he was saved while Tsuneko drowned in the depth of the sea alone (p. 87). The second suicide attempt was trying to overdose himself on sleeping pills (p. 155). The complications of his life have escalated gravely and destructive in a way that he found comfort in his vices which pictures that he is no longer himself and he lost control.

With the obscurity happening in the life of Yozo, Osamu Dazai in his real world was also dwelling in the darkness of numerable vices as his life went downhill. As claimed in his biography, Dazai, after the death of his favorite author, Ryunosuke Akutagawa, did nothing but threw himself into addiction, prostitution, and suicidal attempts. Similar to Yozo, Dazai attempted suicide with a married woman by drowning as well. In addition regarding his failing education, he left the university he was enrolled in without a degree and enrolled in French Literature but failed to attend any lectures ("Famous People").

Moreover, right before his school exams on a cold December night in 1929, he overdosed himself on sleeping pills but the pills he took were not enough to kill him; he survived and graduated after (Thacker 2016).

As the life of Yozo develops in the story, the resemblances of the author's presence solidify as evidences presented profoundly. It can be noticed in the development of the story that the significant escalation of events envelops the plot and projects that the author's presence is indeed found in the progression of the story. Regarding this notion, according to Rossen, there are many different authors who incorporated their personal life in their literary creations where significant events of their lives are integrated as part of the plot of their crafts ("7 Authors Who Wrote Themselves…").

Also, in the development of the story, authors tend to integrate their humane habits, depressing compulsions, lifestyle, and other events in their lives that most authors consciously or unconsciously assimilated into their written literary pieces. Furthermore, not only how the story runs chronologically but also on how the character builds himself that projects a comparable attitude to the author's behavior as well.

In furtherance, the final development of the story is the ending part. In the ending narrative, the life of Oba Yozo became more gravely dangerous as he was hospitalized and rehabilitated in a mental asylum making him feel alienated and invalid as a human being. As evidently accounted on page 166:

> "The young doctor with the bashful smile immediately ushered me to a ward. The key grated in the lock behind me. I was in a mental hospital.
>
> My delirious cry after I swallowed the sleeping pills—that I would go where there were no women— had now materialized in a truly uncanny way: my ward held only male lunatics, and the nurses also were men. There was not a single woman. I was no longer a criminal—I was a lunatic. But no, I was definitely not mad. I have never been mad for even an instant."

It is obvious that the mental health of Oba Yozo deteriorated because his thoughts run strangely as claimed to be a lunatic in this passage. His peculiar behavior was an effect behind his miserable disposition where almost everything was falling apart.

With all the darkness he encountered, news came brought by his brother about his father's death. At that moment of receiving the news, he was struck as if he no longer has the ability to express himself. This scenario was immensely narrated on page 168:

> "The news of my father's death eviscerated me. He was dead, that familiar, frightening presence who had never left my heart for a split second. I felt as though the vessel of my suffering had become empty, as if nothing could interest me now. I had lost even the ability to suffer."

Moreover, after he was released from the mental hospital, he resided in a house in the countryside bought by his elder brother who scrupulously carried out his promise and assumed all the parental responsibilities to Yozo (p.166). The end of story concludes as Yozo breathes in a peaceful place where he still holds himself to have neither happiness nor unhappiness in life as he believed everything will just pass. The depressing critical events in Yozo's life were the mirror that reflects what happened also to Dazai. He suffered from appendicitis and was admitted to a hospital. Because of it, he then developed an addiction to 'Pabinal,' a morphine-based painkiller that deteriorates his mental and physical health ("Famous People").

As his miserable life starts to crumble down, Dazai's elder brother was always on his side taking care of all parental obligations but Dazai no longer considers himself a human being after all the darkness he encountered, he drowned. He was admitted to a mental institution and was forced to resign from using drugs ("Famous People").

In an unfortunate fate, Dazai left the world with complete silence after the publication of his book, No Longer Human. It is conclusive that indeed Yozo's life has the presence of Osamu Dazai because almost all the events in the book are happenings in the reality of Dazai's life story. In all sense, literature is indeed a reflection of anyone's reality and it might be considered fiction, but the story thrives and lives as an unforgotten memory of someone's reality. Moreover, literature brings back old memories and opens up wounds of the past inked in papers to serve as testimonies of human experiences. It is truly accurate that literature is a reflection of one's life and experiences especially authors who integrate their life stories into their literary creations ("The Reflection of Literature").

Seemingly, an author can inevitably integrate his significant experiences into the scenes of his literary work. It is palpably transparent how author the constructs the plot development. The life-changing and crucial episodes of the author's story influence in the making of the development of his literary creation.

As the plot evidently manifests the author's real-life events and experiences, hence, the plot clearly reveals the author's presence.

Characters

Table 2 below is the list of the characters in the novel who potentially possess an authorial presence due to the resemblances the characters bear to the people whom Osamu Dazai met in real life.

Table 2: Characters

CHARACTERS	**AUTHORIAL PRESENCE**
Oba Yozo • The youngest son of a wealthy family • Wide reader • Visually artistic • Alcoholic and was into prostitutes • A morphine addict • Mentally unstable and suicidal	Osamu Dazai • Was the second to the youngest son of a wealthy family • An avid reader of Western literature since childhood • A painter and portraitist • Was also an alcoholic and into prostitutes after Akutagawa's death • Also a morphine addict during a hospitalization

	• Went through multiple suicide attempts
His Father • Was a busy politician	• Osamu Dazai also delved into politics during his university years, particularly Marxism.
Tsuneko • Married • Adulterous • Entertained the idea of dying	• Was married to Hatsuyo Oyama • Adulterous • Attempted suicide multiple times
Masao Horiki • A man with vices, notably drinking and hiring prostitutes. • Was involved in Marxism	• After the death of his writing idol, Ryunosuke Akutagawa, Osamu Dazai's got into a similar range of vices. • Osamu Dazao joined the Japanese Communist Party and became a Marxist.
Takeichi • A classmate of Yozo who had an interest in arts	• Osamu Dazai was exposed to arts since childhood. • He made several artworks ranging from portraits, landscapes, and covers for his magazines.

The author's presence is not just found within the plot as it can also be found in the characters of the story as well. The authorial presence comes in the form of how each character resembles the author either subtly or almost entirely. This form of author's presence has been applied by other authors back then. For example, in Tikaocta's biographical criticism of Edgar Allan Poe's "The Black Cat", he found how the man or the narrator of the said piece was similar to Edgar Allan Poe. Both were married early, alcoholics, and had pets. Some of Poe's experiences were also put in the story ("Biographical Criticism").

Oba Yozo, the main character, and Osamu Dazai, the author of the novel share a similar case to Tikaocta's findings due to the uncanny similarities between the two people bear.

In the novel, Oba Yozo was shown to be a wide reader at a young age as said on page 33.

> "I used to subscribe regularly to a dozen or more children's magazines and for my private reading ordered books of all sorts form Tokyo."

Similarly, Osamu Dazai was an avid reader since childhood. In the translator's introduction of the novel, Donald Keene mentioned that Osamu Dazai was familiar with the arts of the West such as European literature, American movies, including paintings and sculptures (4). In Dazai Museum, it was said that their maid would often visit the family temple every Sunday to borrow books for Dazai to read as it was instructed by his grandmother. He also published his literary works during his high school days and even started a local literary magazine. When he was in college, he enrolled at Tokyo Imperial University taking up French Literature ("Dazai Museum").

Aside from reading, Oba Yozo was also into arts since elementary which were, however, receded when his drawing failed to win people over. This can be seen on page 54 of the novel which says:

> "Ever since elementary school days I enjoyed drawing and looking at pictures. But my pictures failed to win the reputation among my fellow students that my comic stories did"

After meeting Takeichi, his passion for arts was rekindled due to their shared artistic interests as he said so on page 54:

> "I'm going to paint too. I'm going to paint pictures of ghosts and devils and horses out of hell. My voice as I spoke these words to Takeichi was lowered to a barely audible whisper, why I don't know."

When Oba Yozo grew older, he would take on jobs that involved drawing. For example, on page 128, he mentioned how his drawing was no longer just limited to cartoons but to pornography as well.

> "My cartoons were no longer confined to the children's magazines, but now appeared also in the cheap, pornographic magazines that are sold in railway stations."

Osamu Dazai in real life was also into arts. According to Donald Keene in the translator's introduction of the novel, he was already familiar with Western arts both literary and visual (4). The Aomori Museum of Arts also mentioned that Dazai would also make sketches, and self-portraits, including covers for his literary magazines ("Aomori Museum of Arts").

Oba Yozo also started to develop some vices ever since he met Horiki. On page 58, he stated how he was about to immerse himself in the world of vices.

> "Before long a student at the art class was to initiate me into the mysteries of drink, cigarettes, prostitutes, pawnshops and left-wing thought. A strange combination, but it actually happened that way.
>
> "This student's name was Masao Horiki...."

Osamu Dazai also developed a similar set of vices. Unlike Oba Yozo, who developed them after meeting someone, Osamu Dazai developed this due to his grief over the death of an author whom he idolized, Ryunosuke Akutagawa (Yabai 2017).

As the story progressed, Oba Yozo's vices were no longer limited to just smoking, drinking, and hiring prostitutes. He eventually developed an addiction to morphine and became dependent on it whenever he would work. This was evident on pages 163 and 164, respectively.

> "By the time I had come to realize acutely that drugs were as abominable, as foul—no, fouler—than gin, I had already become an out-and-out addict."

"The more I worked the more morphine I consumed, and my debt at the pharmacy reached a frightening figure."

Osamu Dazai also developed an addiction to morphine. This started when he was hospitalized after he attempted to commit suicide for the third time in his apartment in the spring of 1933 (Thacker 2016).

Coupled with his vices and his morphine addiction, Oba Yozo was also emotionally unstable and suicidal. On many occasions, he would often think about wanting to die such as on page 163 when he said "I thought, "I want to die. I want to die more than ever before." On page 87, he committed a double suicide with a woman named Tsuneko but failed.

"We entered the water together. She died. I was saved."

Though there were no records that would elaborately depict how emotionally unstable Dazai was, however, there were records about Osamu Dazai's multiple suicide attempts. In a report done by Thacker of Japan Times (2016), Osamu Dazai attempted to kill himself four times. His first attempt was before his exams via sleeping pills overdose. He, however, survived. His second attempt was with a woman named Tanabe Shimeko. They committed double suicide but only the woman died. In his third attempt, he tried to hang himself in his apartment, but again, he survived and was hospitalized. His fourth attempt was another double suicide with his wife, but they both survived.

Considering how the two – Oba Yozo and Osamu Dazai, resemble each other almost completely, it could be practically assumed that Oba Yozo and Osamu Dazai are one. Goad wrote an article about how authors put themselves in their work. In her example, she mentioned how Oscar Wilde based his character named "Basil" in "The Picture of Dorian Gray" and that his obsession of "Basil" towards "Dorian" was an implication of Oscar Wilde's homosexuality ("Geeks"). The same may be the case between Oba Yozo and Osamu Dazai as both have uncanny resemblance in terms of behavior and the experiences they had.

In the next scrutiny of characters, the study would use Lyon's work to help in locating the authorial presences residing in the characters. In Lyon's "Art is Me: Dazai Osamu's Narrative Self as a Permeable Self", he stated how Dazai's voice was something that can be seen through. He also added how the characters and their respective voices in Dazai's various literary works were telling the readers to merge with Dazai's thoughts (93). Through his work, the study will get an idea about how the characters presented themselves which may be reflective of Osamu Dazai.

Similarly, Malaran also demonstrated in his discussions how the characters represent some people during the time, a piece was written. He made use of Jose Rizal's "Noli Me Tangere" and "El Filibusterismo" as an example. He discussed how characters were reflective to certain groups of people during Rizal's time. As an example, he stated that Crisostomo Ibarra was a representation of the Filipinos who were able to get an education abroad and Padre Damaso represented the abusive priests who were feared yet revered by the people. Through Malaran's example, the study may find how certain characters in Osamu Dazai's "No Longer Human" represent something akin to the author in terms of behavior, if not the people during Dazai's time ("Prezi").

The next character that bears an authorial presence is Oba Yozo's father. Oba Yozo's father in the novel was a politician. On page 70, Oba Yozo said that his father was a member of a political office known as "Diet". There was nothing much about Oba Yozo's father. Not only was he not named, but there were also no specifics about his father's political pursuit other than the idea that he was very busy that he would be away for days as Oba had observed on page 70.

> "Even when my father and I were living in the same house, he was kept so busy receiving guests or going out that sometimes three or four days elapsed without our seeing each other."

Osamu Dazai also got involved in politics, particularly in his university days. According to Sun (2020), Dazai joined the Japanese Communist Party, became a Marxist, and later on left.

Tsuneko bears an authorial presence. In the novel, Tsuneko was a hostess working at a bar in Ginza. On page 79, she mentioned that she was married to a barber who was currently jail for swindling. In spite of her marital status, she entered in an adulterous relationship with Oba Yozo.

> "I've got a husband, you know. He used to be a barber in Hiroshima, but we ran away to Tokyo together at the end of last year. My husband couldn't find a decent job in Tokyo. The next thing I knew he was picked up for swindling someone, and now he's in jail. I've been going to the prison every day, but beginning tomorrow I'm not going anymore."

Lastly, while she may not be as downright suicidal as Oba Yozo, she entertained the idea of dying and agreed to commit double suicide with Oba Yozo which led to her death on page 87.

Osamu Dazai was also married, twice specifically. The first was with a geisha named Oyama Hatsuyo (Cox, 2012) and with Michiko Ishihara (Dazai Museum, n.d.). Dazai was adulterous as he would even be with other women. For example, Dazai engaged in a double suicide with a woman named Tanabe Shimeko while still being married to Hatsuyo. During his marriage with Michiko Ishihara, he had a relationship with a woman named Ota Shizuko. Still married to Michiko Ishihara, Dazai formed an intimate relationship with a woman named Yamazaki Tomie, and committed double suicide together (Cox, 2012).

Masao Horiki also bears an authorial presence. The fact that the two met in an art class would indicate that Horiki was also artistic. However, this was not elaborately shown in the novel as there were no mentions of his artworks as said on page 58. He was also a Marxist and was the one that introduced Oba Yozo to the same political ideology on page 65.

> "...Horiki also took me one day to a secret Communist meeting. (I don't remember exactly what it was called—a "Reading Society," I think.) A secret Communist meeting may have been for Horiki just one more of the sights of Tokyo. I was introduced to the "comrades" and obliged to buy a pamphlet. I then heard a lecture on Marxian economics....."

What Horiki is most notably known for is his immersion in his vices. Horiki was into drinking, smoking, and hiring prostitutes and again, was the one who introduced these to Oba Yozo. His notable indulgence in pleasure-seeking can be notably seen on page 83:

> "I was not particularly fond of Horiki when he played the drunk that way. Horiki knew it, and he deliberately labored the point. "All right? I'm going to kiss her. I'm going to kiss whichever hostess sits next to me. All right?"
>
> "It won't make any difference, I suppose."
>
> "Thanks! I'm starved for a woman."
>
> We got off at the Ginza and walked into the cafe of "wine, women and song."

It has been previously mentioned how visually artistic Osamu Dazai was as well as how he once delved into political activities after joining the Japanese Communist Party and became a Marxist during his university days. In the same phase of his life, he fell into the world of alcohol and hiring prostitutes especially after knowing that the author whom he adored, Ryunosuke Akutagawa, died by committing suicide (Yabai, 2017).

The last character in this discussion that also bears an authorial presence was a boy named Takeichi. Takeichi was a classmate of Oba Yozo during his high school years noted for how he could see through Oba Yozo's pretentions, much to Oba Yozo's fear. On page 53, it was shown that he had an interest in art:

> "I took from my bookshelf a volume of Modigliani reproductions, and showed Takeichi the familiar nudes with skin the color of burnished copper. "How about these? Do you suppose they're ghosts too?"
>
> "They're terrific." Takeichi widened his eyes in admiration. "This one looks like a horse out of hell."
>
> "They really are ghosts then, aren't they?"
>
> "I wish I could paint pictures of ghosts like that," said Takeichi.

Osamu Dazai, though prominently a writer, was a person who was artistic. It was mentioned in the translator's introduction how he was already familiar with Western art. In Aomori Museum of Art, Dazai's artworks were featured which included self-portraits, a rough sketch, some oil paintings, and a cover of his literary magazine called "Memories".

As mentioned previously, there were indeed similarities between the characters and the author in terms of behavior. The findings are similar to how Emily Temple mentioned in her work, "The Art of the Semi-Autobiographical Novel" that the authors integrate themselves in their own works such as when she exemplified an author in the name of Justin Torres based his characters and the story on his own life to conceive his work "We the Animals" ("Flavorwire"). Moreover, Rossen also wrote a work that discussed the authors that applied themselves in their own works. One of the many authors whom he referred to was a man named W. Somerset Maugham who put himself in his works to interact with his characters. Osamu Dazai also performed the same feat, especially considering how he resembled Oba Yozo the most compared to the rest of the characters ("Mental Floss").

The similarities in terms of characteristics that were mentioned above coincided with Osamu Dazai's which proves that the author's presence was found in the characters.

Milieu

Below is Table 3 which presents the author's presence in the milieu more likely the timetable of significant events that highlights a particular time/period.

In order to establish the author's presence in the story's milieu, it is crucial to look for a timeline that is close to and can be compared to the author's real-life stories and events. Malaran's study scrutinizing Jose Rizal Noli Me Tangere testifies author's presence in the milieu. Malaran mentioned that some characters in the novel were a reference to certain people during Rizal's time.

Similarly, in a study conducted by Cole et. al. about William Golding's "Lord of the Flies", they found that the piece was written as an inspiration when the author took part as a naval officer during the Second World War. Looking at the novel's milieu - the location, time, and the events it was made in, an authorial presence can be found. The above table shows the timeline present in the life of the main character, Oba Yozo, which is comparable to the author's real life.

It is apparent how an author could integrate a set or perhaps the entirety of his personality into the characters in the literary work. With that said, these characters are strikingly unique and prominent as they are inspired by or represent a certain aspect of the author or the experiences the author has gone through. The life episodes of the author's experiences play a part in the making of the characters in a literary work to be made.

In the novel, Oba Yozo was shown to be a son of a wealthy family whose father was a prominent politician and landowner in the countryside. His parents were shown to have not much time for him because his elder siblings and his servants acted as a parental figure to him.

Table 3. Milieu

MILIEU	AUTHOR'S PRESENCE
Oba Yozo grew up in a wealthy family.	He was born on June 19, 1909, into a wealthy landowning family in Kanagi, Aomori Prefecture - Northern Japan.
As a child, he was raised by his family's servants.	He was raised by his Aunt Keri, and family servants while his father was working and his mother was ill customarily.
His father died from a gastric ulcer.	His father died from lung cancer on March 4, 1923.
He stayed at his relatives' house for his education.	He moved to a distant relative's house to study at Hirosaki Public Senior High School in 1927.

He met Horiki and his life began to fall apart as he got lost in vices.	In 1927, when his idol Rynosuke Akutagawa, committed suicide he then started to indulge in alcohol and prostitutes.
He was involved in Marxism in the school.	He first encountered Marxism in 1930, but his political commitment resulted in widespread mistrust of all social systems.
He committed double suicide with Tsuneko.	In October 1930, at a beach in Kamakura, Dazai tried to commit a double suicide with Shimeko Tanabe by drowning.
He was rehabilitated in a mental asylum.	In October 1936, he was sent to a mental hospital and was ordered to stop using drugs.

Similarly, Osamu Dazai lives in Kanagi, a remote corner of Japan situated in the Northern tip of Tōhoku in Aomori Prefecture. In his early years, he lived in a newly constructed mansion together with the thirty members of the family. His father was politically involved and his mother was frail and sick.

These lead him to be left under the care of his elder siblings and servants. They also bore similarities in their upbringing due to the almost absence of their parents. Later in the story, Oba learned from his brother that their father had died of gastric ulcer. There was no other information about Oba Yozo's father in the novel. The same Osamu Dazai's father, there was not much detail about him other than the fact that he was a politician who died of lung cancer on March 4, 1923. Despite subtle distinctions, both fathers had such a strong similarity to one another that Osamu Dazai was able to bring his encounters with his father into the novel.

In the same manner, an essay entitled "Biographical Approach To Kate Chopin's "The Story Of An Hour" (n.a., 2016) took a similar approach to the literary work being studied, namely "The Story Of An Hour." According to the study, the main character of the story, Louise Mallard, bore similarities and resembled Kate Chopin, the novel's author. One of the examples is the death of the main character's husband, which may have been a reference to Kate Chopin's mother being widowed. The author's milieu may have also been another reason why the literary piece was created.

Moreover, Oba Yozo was left in the care of his distant relative's family, whose house was so close to the high school he attended. Even after the morning bell had rung he could still make it to his class in time if he ran. That was his first experience living in a strange town he found it far more agreeable than staying in their native place. Comparably, Osamu Dazai enrolled in Aomori Prefectural High School in 1925 and lived at the home of a distant relative, Tazaemon Toyoda, while in school. In 1927, he enrolled in Hirosaki Public Senior High School, and while there, he lived at the home of another distant cousin, Toyosaburo Fujita.

When Oba Yozo gets more and more immersed in the art world, he encounters Horiki Masao, his male friend who introduced and exposed him to drugs, alcohol, and prostitutes. Oba was also involved in Marxism. In the novel, Oba Yozo claims that there are Marxists of all kinds. Some, like Hiroki, coined the term "modernity" to describe themselves. Others, such as Oba Yozo, were drawn to the movement by its stench of irrationality. He went on to say that if actual Marxists had found what Horiki and Oba were truly interested in, they would have been enraged and expelled them and driven them out immediately as vile traitors. Similarly, when Dazai's favorite writer Rynosuke Akutagawa committed suicide in 1927, Dazai's life started to change. He began to disregard his academics, splurging on clothing, drinking, and prostitutes with his allowance. He was also interested in Marxism, which was repressed by the government at that time.

Furthermore, there are significant occurrences in Yozo's life that closely resemble Dazai's reality. Oba Yozo and Tsuneko, a married hostess with whom he had an affair after meeting at a Ginza bar, decided to commit double suicide in the sea near Kamakura. Tsuneko, on the other hand, died as a result of the crime, leaving Oba Yozo as the sole survivor. This exacerbated his trauma and suffering, which has been there for years. Similarly, while married to Hatsuyo, Osamu Dazai had an affair with Tanabe Shimeko, a nineteen-year-old waitress in Ginza. They also committed double suicide, killing Tanabe Shimeko but leaving Dazai alive. Both have an adulterous affair that leads to a double suicide and the death of the ladies involved.

After that incident, Oba resumed drinking and developed a morphine addiction, and was eventually isolated for rehabilitation. It was stated in the novel that he was placed in a mental hospital. And that a young doctor ushered him to the ward and the key was granted in the lock behind him. He added in the statement that his ward held only male lunatics, and the nurses also were men. There was not a single woman. Similarly, Osamu Dazai, before his third suicide attempt in 1935, suffered from appendicitis and was admitted to a hospital. There, he developed an addiction to 'Pabinal,' a morphine-based painkiller. After battling his addiction, he was sent and admitted to a mental hospital in October 1936, where he was isolated in a room and forced to stop using drugs.

It is evident that authors integrate the milieu they grew up in their literary works, especially in cases that are semi-autobiographical in nature. If scrutinized extensively enough, it could be evident in the way how the author constructs the characters, setting, and even how the story progresses reflect in the author's milieu.

The above-mentioned events of Oba Yozo and Osamu Dazai's timeline prove how the author's milieu influences the development of the literary work.

Summary Of Findings, Conclusion, And Recommendations

This chapter presents the summary of findings in answer to the sub-problems raised and arrives at a conclusion based on these findings. With the findings and conclusion taken into account, basic recommendations to the beneficiaries of the study are prescribed.

Summary of Findings

The findings of the study are as follows:

1. As the plot evidently manifests the author's real-life events and experiences, hence, the plot clearly reveals the author's presence.

2. The similarities in terms of characteristics were matched to Osamu Dazai which proves that the author's presence was found in the characters.

3. The events of Oba Yozo and Osamu Dazai's timeline prove how the author's milieu influences the development of the literary work.

Conclusion

Based on the findings of the study, Osamu Dazai's novel No Longer Human reveals the author's presence.

Recommendations

Due to the limitations of the study, the following recommendations are endorsed:

1. Extensive exploration of the structural development of the plot using other plot models

2. Probe into the characters' psychological aspects especially their motivations, desires, and influences that drive depravity.

3. In-depth investigation of the different kinds of milieu of the novel and its relevance to the theme of the story.

Further Studies

1.	The Study of Moral Implications found in Paulo Coelho's The Alchemists

2.	Dean Koontz's The Voice of the Night: A Psychological Study

3.	The Authorial Presence in J.K Rowling's Select Harry Potter Sequel

Works Cited

Abrams and Harpham. "A Glossary of Literary Terms" 9th ed.,Wadsworth, 2009.

file:///C:/Users/pc/Downloads/Glossary_of_LITERARY_TERMS.pdf Accessed 20 Nov. 2020

"Biographical Approach to Chopin's "The Story of an Hour"."*StudyMoose* ,22 Sep 2016,

https://studymoose.com/biographical-approach-to-kate-chopins-the-story-of-an hour-essay.Accessed 6 Dec. 2020.

"Biographical Criticism: To Build a Fire by Jack London."*PhDessay.com*, 9 Aug 2016,

https://phdessay.com/biographical-criticism-to-build-a-fire-by-jack-london/.Accessed 6 Dec. 2020.

Boer, Lianne. "Narratives of Force: The Presence of the Writer in International Legal

Scholarship."*Netherlands International Law Review, Springer International Publishing*, 1 Jan. 1999, https://link.springer.com/article/10.1007/s40802-019-00131-9 .Accessed 5 Dec. 2020.

Claassen, Eefje, et al. "Author Representations in Literary Reading." *John Benjamins*

Publishing Catalog, John Benjamins Publishing Company, 15 Feb. 2012, https://www.jbeplatform.com/content/books/9789027274939 Accessed 25 Nov. 2020

Cole, Ahleahet. al."Applying Biographical Criticism to The Lord of the Flies" *Sutori*,

www.sutori.com/story/applying-biographical-criticism-to-the-lord-of-the-flies--wbxB2JaffLrVLH2yDobojwgm .Accessed 6 Dec. 2020.

Dontcheva-Navratilova, Olga."Authorial presence in academic discourse: Functions of author-referencepronouns" *Research Gate*, January 2013.https://www.researchgate.net/publication/286885760_Authorial_presence_in_academic_discourse_Functions_of_author-reference_pronouns. Accessed 4 Dec. 2020

Fenster, Mark. "Constructing the Image of Authorial Presence: David O. Selznick and the Marketing of Since You Went Away." Journal of Film and Video, vol. 41, no. 1, 1989, pp. 36–51. *JSTOR*, www.jstor.org/stable/20687848.Accessed 1 Dec. 2020.

Ferguson, Suzanne. "The Face in the Mirror: Authorial Presence in the Multiple Vision of

Third-Person Impressionist Narrative." *Criticism*, vol. 21, no. 3, 1979, pp. 230–250. *JSTOR*, www.jstor.org/stable/23102630. Accessed 12 Dec. 2020

Freeman, Margaret."Authorial Presence in Poetry."*Scribd*, Scribd, www.scribd.com/document/369251754/Authorial-Presence-in-Poetry?fbclid=IwAR0qfurQ4OaLm8b_51LWmW6zTqfr6S84z8CQpfKE8jG54xJnqK0HZx1Mm0Accessed 25 Nov. 2020

Goad, Poppy."How Far Do Authors Reflect Themselves in Their Protagonists?" *Geeks*, 2018,https://vocal.media/geeks/how-far-do-authors-reflect-themselves-in-their-protagonists-1 Accessed 6 Dec. 2020

Guerin et. al."A Handbook of Critical Approaches to Literature"5th ed.,Oxford University

Press,2005.https://uogbooks.files.wordpress.com/2014/10/wilfred_l-guerin_earle_labor_lee_morgan_jeannbokos-z1.pdf Accessed 20 Nov. 2020

Lord, Richard. *How tragic novel by suicidal writer Osamu Dazai informs a Hong Kong* artist's 'comical' work. 2018. https://www.scmp.com/magazines/post-magazine/books/article/2169251/how-tragic-novel-suicidal-writer-osamu-dazai-informs Accessed on 6 Dec. 2020

"Life as a Writer - Knowing Osamu Dazai - Dazai Museum." 日本, http://dazai.or.jp/en/knowing/writer.html Accessed 8 Jun. 2021

Malaran, Denson. "Historical and Biographical Approach."*SlideShare*, 4 September 2017, www.slideshare.net/DensonMalaran/historical-and-biographical-approach Accessed 6 Dec. 2020.

Mallon, Thomas, and Adam Kirsch. "When We Read Fiction, How Relevant Is the Author's Biography?" *The New York Times*, 24 June 2014, www.nytimes.com/2014/06/29/books/review/when-we-read-fiction-how-relevant-is-the-authors-biography.html .Accessed 6 Dec. 2020

"Osamu Dazai: A Great Japanese Author with a Tragic Life: YABAI - The Modern, Vibrant Face of Japan." *YABAI*,http://dazai.or.jp/en/knowing/writer.htmlyabai.com/p/3137.Accessed June 8, 2021

Pankenier, Sara. "'Uncle Lighthouse': The Authorial Presence in Vladimir Maiakovskii's

Books for Children." The Princeton University Library Chronicle, vol. 68, no. 3, 2007, pp. 909–940. *JSTOR*, www.jstor.org/stable/10.25290/prinunivlibrchro.68.3.0909.Accessed 24 Nov. 2020.

Rodriguez, Emily. Osamu Dazai. Encyclopedia Britannica. June 15, 2020.

https://www.britannica.com/biography/Dazai-Osamu?fbclid=IwAR3zzgfaFixzHEbe80zNZkbJYMTmWVW_YJb0U75k_QKFrAab0vWFoJ71YbY Accessed 13 Jan. 2021

Rossen, Jake. "7 Authors Who Wrote Themselves into Their Work."*Mental Floss*, 9 Mar. 2016, www.mentalfloss.com/article/60290/7-authors-who-wrote-themselves-their-work .Accessed 6 Dec. 2020

Sarig, Gissi. "Literate Texts, Articulating Selves: Qualities of Author's Presence"

SpringerLink,https://link.springer.com/article/10.1023/A:1013812828396?fbclid=IwAR2fFLcG5m9i0DMHMMpkSFJ-VCGgzAyT_zIiMjqVF7ORiHc9ergbxGU0Ubk .Accessed 24 Nov. 2020.

Sun, Jiacheng."Research on Osamu Dazai"PSU, February 7, 2020, http://personal.psu.edu/jzs375/Osamu_Dazai%20page.html.Accessed June 8, 2021

Tang and Suganthi. "The 'I' in Identity: Exploring Writer Identity in Student Academic Writing through the First Person Pronoun."*Englishfor Specific Purposes*, 30 Nov. 1998, https://eric.ed.gov/?id=EJ593221 .Accessed 1 Dec. 2020

Temple, Emily. "The Art of the Semi-Autobiographical Novel."*Flavorwire*, Flavorwire, 18 Nov. 2011, https://www.flavorwire.com/232976/the-art-of-the-semi-autobiographical-novel. Accessed 6 Dec. 2020

Thacker, Eugene. "Black Illumination: the Disqualified Life of Osamu Dazai." *The Japan Times*, 30 Apr. 2016, www.japantimes.co.jp/culture/2016/03/26/books/black-illumination-disqualified-life-osamu-dazai/.Accessed June 8, 2021

Tikaocta."Historical – Biographical Approach of 'The Black Cat.'"*KATA TIKA*, 16 Dec. 2015, https://semuatentangtika.wordpress.com/2015/08/07/the-black-cat/6 Dec. 2020 "Who Was Osamu Dazai? Everything You Need to Know." – *Facts, Childhood, Family Life, Achievements & Death*, www.thefamouspeople.com/profiles/osamu-dazai-16872.php.Accessed June 8, 2021

Wood. "Author's characters and the character of the author: The typical in fiction" *Research Gate*, September 2011,https://www.researchgate.net/publication/271383104_Author's_characters_and_the_character_of_the_author_The_typical_in_fiction .Accessed 6 Dec. 2020

Appendices

APPENDIX A
THE AUTHOR'S BACKGROUND

OSAMU DAZAI

A Japanese author, Osamu Dazai, was born on June 19, 1909, and died on June 13, 1948. He is considered one of Japan's leading fiction writers of the 20th century. He began to emerge at the end of World War II.

A number of his most notable works are considered modern-day classics in Japan, such as The Setting Sun (Shayō) and No Longer Human (Ningen Shikkaku). Dazai's tales have captivated the hearts of many readers with a semi-autobiographical style and openness with his personal life.

The life of Dazai was tragic and absurd the same with the depiction of life in his stories. His 1948 novel "No Longer Human" is still one of the most popular books in
modern Japanese literature. It has gained quite a few adaptations of Dazai's literary work. All of his stories have been translated by Donald Keene.

Osamu Dazai, committed suicide several times. The first one took place on a cold December night in 1929, just before his exams at school. However, the sleeping pill he took was not sufficient; he survived and graduated. The second time was in October 1930, it was a double suicide with a young woman he barely knew on the barren sands of a beach in Kamakura. Sadly, the woman died while Dazai was rescued by a passing fishing boat. He moved on and got married and began a writing career. In the spring of 1933, a third attempt was made: he tried to hang himself from a beam in the mesmerizing stillness of his Tokyo apartment. Once again, although he was hospitalized and acquired a morphine addiction, Dazai survived. And the fourth was when Dazai and his wife, attempted a double suicide in the fall of 1936, but still they were alive. Dazai committed suicide in 1948 after several unsuccessful attempts earlier in his life, leaving a novel ominously entitled Goodbye unfinished.

Ryūnosuke Akutagawa, Murasaki Shikibu, and Fyodor Dostoyevsky were among his influences. While Dazai is still widely celebrated in Japan, with only a handful of his works available in English, he remains fairly unknown in other countries. His most popular work outside of Japan is his last novel, No Longer Human.

APPENDIX B

NO LONGER HUMAN SUMAMARY

The story consisted of three chapters ranging from his childhood days to his late 20's. The first notebook or memorandum is during his childhood days where he says everyone around him as egotistic which he could not comprehend. He then resorted to clownery to develop some relationships with everyone. It was also in this chapter where it was implied that he was sexually abused.

The second notebook was around his high school and university days. There he met Takeichi who could see through Oba's actions which made him disturbed in return. He then befriended Takeichi as a measure. He also discovered a talent in painting which he found better in expressing things. In his university days, he became academically neglecting. After meeting Horiki in an art class, he got into various vices such as drinking, smoking and prostitution. This is where he also committed a double-suicide with someone at a one-night stand which lead to just him surviving alone.

In his third notebook, he was expelled from the university he was in. He met a widower with a child and tried to have a relationship with them. Later on, he left them and went to look for some meaning in his self in the society. He then met a naive and young Yoshiko whom she agreed to share a relationship with him in the condition that he was to stop his vices.

He started to live well because of Yoshiko and even had a job. Horiki, however, showed up awakened Oba's unhealthy tendencies once again. This was worsened when he saw Yoshiko was sexually assaulted by a neighbor who led him to feel distant towards her.

He then became an alcoholic and developed an addiction to morphine due to the incident. Eventually, he was remotely admitted to a mental institution and eventually someplace else away from people for rehabilitation. This was when started to feel alien from the society.

About the author

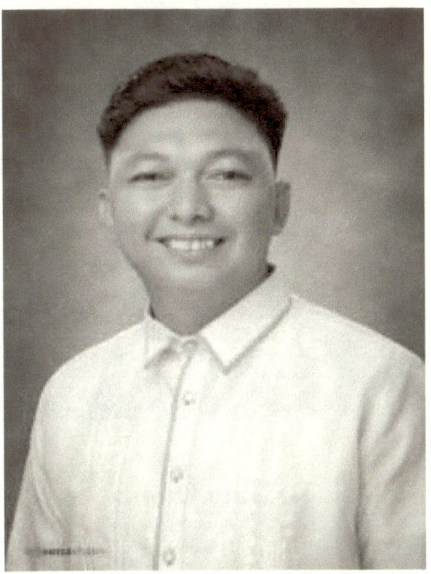

Louren Jay Caballero

LOUREN JAY CABALLERO is a Bachelor of Arts in Literature Magna Cum Laude graduate from Cebu Normal University. He was a college council officer for three consecutive years in the same institution and a member of Elite and Drama Society – an accredited college department organization. He was a freelance content writer and online tutor during the two years of the pandemic. Now, he currently teaches in a private school in Cebu, Philippines as a Senior High School teacher. He joined several writing competitions and hailed triumphs in some of them. He attended workshops relevant to literature and poetry to strengthen his craft, to fortify his skills, and learn methods for writing effective stories. As per him, in his voyage to creativity, he will always be an apprentice of life and literature. Though he is still searching for his voice, literature will always be his driving force in expressing his passion, translating his ideas into works of letters and art, and dripping his creative sentences through written and spoken poetry. The course of his dream to become an author, known by many, shall remain the pinnacle of his aim. And this is all for the love of literature.

Dr. Lito Diones

DR. LITO L. DIONES is a passionate and family-oriented person. He is a professor, both in the undergraduate and graduate schools at Cebu Normal University, handling Literature, Research, Communication, and Theater subjects. He has been in the teaching profession for more or less 30 years, and half of it was spent in a private school in Cebu City, Philippine Christian Gospel School. With his years of experience at Cebu Normal University, he handled the Theater and Communication subjects for 10 years which led to write his first book co-authored by other colleagues titled Speech and Theater Arts. He acquired his undergraduate education at Silliman University in Dumaguete City and both his master's and doctorate degrees were finished at Cebu Normal University. Sir Bem, as he is fondly called by his students, is an educator, researcher, performer, and artist.

Mark Paul Famat

MARK PAUL FAMAT is a Bachelor of Arts in Literature Magna Cum Laude graduate from Cebu Normal University. He is a zealous person in writing poetry and crafting visual art. He draws portraits for leisure. As he is shy in nature, he dwells and wanders in reading, which led him to be a wide reader of literature. Besides that, he is philosophical. He often questions everything and his curiosity about things is immeasurable. In addition, his passion for music bleeds in his mastery of playing the keyboard. His life is a piece of music. A tune of a thriving individual, enduring and seizing life, as all of us should be.

Christia Mae Rodriguez

CHRISTIA MAE RODRIGUEZ is a graduate of Bachelor of Arts in Literature from Cebu Normal University. She is currently working as a College Instructor at ACLC College of Mandaue. She is also the adviser of Iskriptura Publication, an accredited school organization in ACLC. She began writing in high school as a correspondent for her school's student publication. At that moment, she wasn't yet into literary writing as she is more focused on journalistic writing. But it was in Senior High School that she started to write novelettes, poems, and short stories. She is a writer-contributor of Viva Psicom Publishing and Kabisdak Literary Lighthouse, her published works are mostly short stories and poems. She is a fellow Mugna Creative Writing and a Member of Bathalad Sugbo, a literary organization in the Philippines. Her research interests are Literary Studies and Cultural Studies.

www.ingramcontent.com/pod-product-compliance
Lightning Source LLC
LaVergne TN
LVHW041225080526
838199LV00083B/3360